The Revised Bible

for our troubled times

Rupert Butcher

ISBN 9979-8-2744-0134-0

For dinosaurs and benighted heathens everywhere.

Contents   Page

Old Testament

Contents   Page

New Testament

Biblical Aid

Old Testament

From The Beginning until Television

14 billion years ago, God leaves a gigantic knife in the microwave which causes a Big Bang.

4.5 billion years ago, the Devil lights a cigarette whilst the gas is on, which results in the Solar System.

3.8 billion years ago, God creates single cell organisms that reproduce through mitosis.

2 billion years ago, the Devil retaliates by creating sexual reproduction.

240 million years ago, God creates dinosaurs.

66 million years ago, God is fed up with dinosaurs so fires a meteor into Mexico.

62 million years ago, during the Summer of Love, God begins to create duck billed platypuses.

10 million years ago, the Devil creates Asian tree mosquitoes (which are the worst kind).

In 1925, God creates television.

In 1982, the Devil creates shopping channels.

Marriage

Humans should only marry other humans.

Animals do not have the language skills to consent, do not look good in wedding clothes and do not normally have enough money for weddings.

Weddings are important because you will only have a few of them in your life. Celebrities have more weddings than non-celebrities because they are more important.

First weddings are usually the most expensive, have lots of guests and as many unicorns as credit providers will allow.

Final weddings are often more casual, with only witnesses as guests and have no unicorns because credit providers do not allow additional unicorns on hire purchase until earlier unicorns are paid off.

Adam and Eve in God's Greenhouse

One winter, God entrusts Adam and Eve with watering his vast collection of plants when he goes on a snowboarding holiday. He instructs them not to smoke any of his plants whilst he is away.

After a few days, Eve begins to wonder why these plants are forbidden. She suggests smoking one tiny bit and Adam, easily influenced, agrees. This leads to smoking a medium sized bit of plant, and then a bigger bit of plant, and then a really big bit of plant. By the time God returns, they have smoked all his plants and eaten all his Wotsits. God is furious and banishes them from his greenhouse.

Adam and Eve live knowing that they have let God down and have to learn to grow plants on their own. Their plants are never as good as the ones in God's greenhouse.

Noah's Space Ark

Global warming causes significant flooding which threatens life on Earth. Noah, a scientist and billionaire, seeks to prolong humanity's survival by colonising other planets.

He fills his Space Ark with 100,000 humans, which would alleviate inbreeding, but calculates that there is insufficient room for animals. Thus, those aboard must satisfy their need for animal companionship with Tamagotchis. Food production cargo includes: 600,000 tomato seeds, 30,000,000,000,000 chicken cells, 30,000,000,000,000 cow cells, 580,000 corn seeds, 15,000,000 wheat seeds, 1,400,000 soybean seeds, 1000 crickets, 870,000 peanut seeds, 145,000 sweet potato slips and 2,000,000 vegan sausages.

After colonising several planets, Noah observes that the rainbow colours on Earth's oceans resemble a safe balance of phytoplankton and carbon for the floods to have stopped. Space Ark safely returns to Earth. And whenever survivors see a rainbow, they are reminded of how disgusting food was aboard Space Ark and make sure they look after their planet.

Tower of Babel and Mobile Phones

The great Tower of Babel transmits data for mobile phones programmed in Babblish++.

Babblish++ is named after the Babblish language, which is a simplified form of English and emojis that dominates human communication.

God is fed up with lazy and apathetic humans on their phones: doom scrolling, watching Bikbok videos and overusing the eggplant emoji. So, he tries to destroy the Tower with an AK47. His attempt fails so he just smites it with fire, bible style.

Humans are devastated because their mobile phones do not work. In order to communicate, they have to develop languages of their own, learn to read and write, and create paper items called books. This is hard work and incredibly time consuming. Stupid God!

Abraham, Sarah and Sex Education

Abraham and Sarah are withdrawn from sex education in school and are told that being naked is a sin. After they are married, they sleep in separate beds and are always dutifully clothed in front of one another.

They try to get pregnant by praying, reading the bible and preaching, but with no success. So, they pray harder, read the bible more intensely and preach more passionately. Still, no baby appears.

Whilst wistfully discussing their dilemma in a cafe, Sarah notices a children's book on the floor called, 'How babies are made'. She picks it up and begins reading. She shows it to Abraham who, after the initial shock, becomes excited by the 'graphic' illustrations.

Four minutes later, a tiny sperm fertilises a tiny egg and then Abraham and Sarah share a cigarette.

The Binding of Isaac to Marry his Cousin

God insists that Abraham's son, Isaac, marries his cousin Rebecca. Isaac protests as he feels he is too young to get married, thinks marrying his cousin is weird, and suspects that he is more interested in men than women. Despite this, Abraham, determined to prove his love for God, forces Isaac to announce the engagement and begins extensive wedding planning. God is pleased.

At last, the wedding day arrives. Just before Bridal Chorus plays, God texts Abraham to say that he is satisfied with Abraham's loyalty and that Isaac does not have to marry Rebecca. Abraham leaps towards the altar, throws Isaac's corsage on the floor and tells Isaac that he may live freely and experiment as he wishes, within reason. No animals.

Rebecca is relieved too. She loves horses more than she could love any man.

Jacob Catfished by Leah and Rachel

Sisters, Leah and Rachel are both at an age where they should consider settling down. Leah is older than Rachel so their father wants Leah settled first.

Rachel has a beautiful smile, sparkling eyes and a superb figure. Her sister Leah has a great personality.

Their father puts pictures of Rachel on a dating app to capture the attention of Jacob, an eligible bachelor. However, when Jacob goes on the date, it is Leah who shows up. Whilst annoyed by the deception, Jacob does not pass up the opportunity to avoid going home alone.

Jacob searches for the real Rachel and eventually finds and marries her. However, he still sleeps with Leah on the side because, after all, she has a great personality.

Baby Moses Rescued on the River

Moses is a famous baby model. He has symmetrical features and models hats, nappies and most of all, baskets.

One advert is being filmed on a river. Just as the soothing voice says, 'The basket that keeps your baby safe', Moses and the basket veer down a separate stream that leads to rapids and a crocodile lake.

The film crew ring emergency services. Police Inspector Maris is nearby in her helicopter. She is a silver medal Olympic swimmer, has a black belt in Judo and achieved a double first in Anthropology and Helicopter Pilot Training. She excelled in her Child Protection course and is the only known police officer to have a completely clean background check, including never having dodged a train fare or put Pink Lady apples through self-checkouts as Royal Gala apples.

She flies the helicopter towards the stream, dives into a waterfall, swims across rapids, hip throws a small crocodile into a thorny bush and rescues Moses.

She receives a bravery award. The Department of Social Work remove Moses from his current guardians and send him to live with Maris.

Plagues after Fifa

At times, God gets angry, often after losing at Fifa to the Devil, and consequently sends plagues to Earth.

These have included:

- Call centre automation
- Reality TV
- Buffering
- Flat earthers
- Comic sans
- Seagulls
- Psychics
- The M25
- Live laugh love merchandise
- Prime ministers from Eton

Samson, Delilah and Love Island

Samson and Delilah are arguably the most famous Love Island contestants. Samson is tall, athletic and has gorgeous hair, and is instantly attracted to the glamourous and charismatic Delilah.

One island challenge takes place in a lion park. A jealous contestant pushes Samson into the lion pit. The lions look over. They are a bit annoyed about being woken up. Then, they go back to sleep.

Surviving this makes Samson arrogant and annoying. He becomes very drunk and obnoxious one night. So, when he is asleep, Delilah shaves his hair and eyebrows. The next day, Samson is a laughingstock.

Humiliated and angry, Samson punches holes in the walls of the house, which is cheaply constructed and mostly made of plasterboard. The house collapses. All the contestants survive but the plaster dust ruins their hair forever. They are no longer considered beautiful.

Moses, The Burning Bush and Waitrose

Some unruly teenagers set fire to a bush. Moses puts out the fire and realises he needs to help these troubled youths if the neighbourhood is ever to get a Waitrose.

So, he sets out to hug a teenager every day. The teenagers are so touched at being hugged that they stop setting fire to things. Eventually, Waitrose opens a shop in the neighbourhood... The Devil builds an American Candy Store next door.

The 10 Commandments

God gives Moses 10 commandments on top of a double decker bus:

Thou shalt respect the queuing etiquette.
Thou shalt not tailgate despite driving a BMW.
Thou shalt honour the round system in public houses.
Thou shalt not put apostrophes in plurals.
Thou shalt not talk through films.
Thou shalt replace the toilet paper.
Thou shalt not feign injury during football matches.
Thou shalt use headphones for listening to music in public.
Thou shalt not leave sparkling wine in the freezer.
Thou shalt not cut down thy neighbour's wife's tree.

Moses Parts Sea with Jet Skis

Unscrupulous potters produce commemorative ashtrays for a royal wedding. They are popular amongst the general public as well as smokers but, they are banned locally for being vulgar.

Bordering countries recognise that the ashtrays represent a great commercial opportunity.

Moses supports the freedom of consumer rights and leads shoppers to his secret stash of jet skis. This allows them to cross the sea and buy royal ashtrays from a variety of vendors.

Soon, the ashtrays become so prevalent amongst the community that authority figures turn a blind eye to any breach of the Royal Ashtray Law.

The David and Goliath Game

David and Goliath is the most popular VR game available. Players, in the role of Dave the shepherd, are on a mission to defeat Goliath, a narcissistic and badly behaved giant, whose creation is the result of an unusual chlamydia variant growing on enriched uranium.

Ideally, players should only use a staff, sling and five stones to defeat Goliath. Most players spend time finding suitable stones and perfecting their slingshot skills. Others spend time walking on the lands of Elah and looking after sheep.

Daniel, Foreign Cars and the Lions' Den

Tariffs on foreign cars quadruple very suddenly. Daniel really wants a foreign car so he flies abroad, buys one, then drives it home.

Soon after, he accidentally reverses into a tax inspector's car and his tax evasion attempt is exposed during the insurance claim.

He is sentenced to a night in the lions' den which is located near a motorway.

That evening, another tax evader is driving a lorry full of smuggled cat food past the den. He crashes and all the cat food spills out into the den. The lions are delighted... They hardly ever have foie gras cat food for dinner.

Daniel leaves the den unharmed and the tax inspector drops the insurance claim and the pursuit of unpaid tax, in return for the foreign car.

Jonah and the Whale's Teeth

Jonah works for a fizzy drinks company. God is concerned that the drinks are causing tooth decay and rising sugar levels in the ocean. He gives Jonah an ultimatum to reduce the drinks' sugar content within 40 days. Jonah contacts his superiors who give him a 96 page 'Recipe Change Request' form along with 144 pages of 'Easy Read Guidance Notes'.

The form requires details of all pre and post recipe ingredients. Jonah researches molecular diagrams for sucrose, high fructose corn syrup, glucose, aspartame, acesulfame K, phosphoric acid and citrus acid. He struggles to remember his high school chemistry and to distinguish sweeteners from sugars, so he never actually completes the form.

After 40 days, God punishes Jonah by making him brush a whale's teeth. This particular whale had been drinking lots of fizzy beverages as well as fish smoothies. It takes Jonah 3 smelly days to scrape off all the plaque and floss properly.

Jonah completes the form, and the company reduces the amount of sugar in their drinks. Consumers dislike the new low sugar drinks and so the company quickly reinstates their old recipe.

New Testament

Virgin Mary in an Open Relationship

Mary and Joseph are in an open relationship. After feeling a bit sick one morning, Mary realises she has muddled up her combined pill and seaweed vitamin tablets.

Mary tells Joseph that she is pregnant but does not know who the father is. He is annoyed.

Mary gives him some space and goes to collect their car, which regularly breaks down and is being repaired. She tells Gabriel, the mechanic, about her dilemma and he promises her that all will be fine. He also points out that previously, their relationship was slightly more open on Joseph's side than hers, to alleviate any guilt that she may feel.

And as promised, Joseph is soon ok with everything and their car never breaks down again.

They decide to raise the child in a more conventional setting in Bethlehem, where no one could gossip about their past.

The Birth of Jesus and a Farmer

Joseph and Mary drive to Bethlehem. All the reasonable hotels are booked because Taylor Swift is performing there that weekend. So, they have to stay in a Premier Inn.

Mary goes into labour. There is no time to go to hospital. She has no access to pain relief which is ironic because she has been pro drugs for most of her adult life.

Fortunately, a farmer is also staying in the hotel with his animals. He helps deliver the baby. He puts his hand into Mary. Easy. Just like lambing. The baby is born and named Jesus Christ or JC for short.

There is a Mensa conference in the hotel. Three members visit JC and bring gifts: a Nintendo, a Disney+ subscription and some Silly Putty.

Christmas

Christmas is an important time for Christians because there are opportunities to indulge in excessive consumerism, outlandish decorations and cringey work parties.

Sofas are always on sale at this time of year. This is because Christians often buy a new Christmas sofa for guests, both invited and uninvited, to enjoy.

Card giving is popular. Christians often write their pets' names on cards which makes Christians feel happy. The pets do not care.

Watching television is popular at Christmas. Viewers select simple shows that they have seen many times before so that there are no surprises. However, watching the new John Lewis advert is always exciting.

The key to enjoying Christmas Day is to remain in a continuous state of mild inebriation without being so drunk that you burn dinner. Because it is cold at Christmas time, Christians often drink champagne cocktails. To make a champagne cocktail, put two tablespoons of brandy, two drops of Angostura bitter and half a teaspoon of brown sugar in a glass, then top up with champagne.

John the Baptist and Swimming

John the Baptist is really into bushcraft and outdoorsy activities. He drives land rovers and wears clothes from North Face. He teaches Jesus how to fish, hunt and make fire from sticks.

One day, they go swimming and Jesus thanks John because he feels truly enthralled by nature and has a headrush from the cold water. Jesus later adds 'wild swimming' to his online dating profile.

Jesus's Digital Detox in the Desert

Jesus acknowledges his debilitating addiction to his phone so goes on a digital detox retreat in the desert for 40 days and 40 nights.

During a camel ride, the Devil appears with a phone and tempts Jesus with a video of an orange president saying something really, really, really stupid. Jesus resists. Whilst Jesus is rolling down sand dunes, the Devil reappears and tries to lure in Jesus with a new dating app that uses quantum mechanics to find your perfect match. Jesus supresses his curiosity and enjoys the freedom of the sand. The Devil then coaxes Jesus with photos of celebrities who were thin, then fat, then thin again. Jesus resists and continues mindfulness painting.

The Devil tempts Jesus with kitten videos, how to get curly hair in 30 minutes and five block Tetris. Jesus defies all temptation.

After 40 days and 40 nights, Jesus receives his digital detox completion certificate, and his phone is returned. He vows to only use it for: work, banking, shopping, emails, booking holidays, messaging friends and the occasional funny cat video.

Jesus Turns Water into Wine post Brexit

Jesus discreetly buys enormous quantities of wine in anticipation that Brexit would limit the availability of decent wine.

He and his family are guests at a wedding. A lack of HGV drivers means that wine supplies are low and diminishing quickly. Jesus's mother persuades him to fetch wine from his secret reserves.

Jesus leaves the dinner table, saying that he needs some water. He quietly signals to some waiters and they all go to collect wine from his secret cellar.

They return to the wedding with many cases of reasonable quality wine. Everyone is overwhelmed by Jesus's generosity. The celebrations continue long into the night and everyone is happy. Until the next day, when they are hungover, and the lack of HGV drivers means bacon supplies are also low.

The Good Samaritan during Covid

A pandemic results in many people being in need. A lingerie-designing baroness deceives the public and embezzles £200 million. A prime minister ignores the crisis and has a party in his garden. A president flouts advice and suggests drinking bleach.

Fortunately, some scientists develop vaccines and medical staff work long and difficult shifts. They are rewarded with pots and pans being banged in their honour.

Jesus Walking on Water

Jesus and Peter walk through shallow waters to a tiny island, where the main attraction is watching seagulls use items they have stolen from the mainland. A little later, the water has risen slightly so Jesus checks his tide app and walks back. Peter is having too much fun watching some seagulls assemble flat pack furniture, so he decides to stay. Besides, he doesn't really have much faith in tide apps.

Peter soon realises that it is high tide, and that he is stranded. He phones Jesus, who runs to get the coast guards. The coast guards are fed up with people not checking the tide app and getting stuck on the island so they said Peter would have to stay there.

Peter has an uncomfortable night on the island sharing an old tent with some seagulls and their leftover kebabs. He walks back the next day. Jesus consoles him by writing a song about the event called Walking on Water. The song is rubbish but somehow teenagers like it and it makes it into the top ten. Peter subsequently decides to use and trust tide apps.

The Last Supper and Far Right Politics

Jesus hosts curry night one Friday.

After dinner, they play *'Far Right Politics – The nastiest game since Cards Against Humanity'*. One player reads an incident card then others read their response cards. The incident reading player selects the funniest response.

Matthew reads an incident: *'There's been a tsunami'*. Responses include: *'Immigrants will block the M4'*, *'Put them on disused oil rigs'*, *'Foreign languages are scary'*, *'Racism is a right'*, but the winning card is, *'Paint over Mickey Mouse'*.

After many rounds, Peter reads the final incident: *'Homelessness is on the rise'*. Jesus and Judas are neck and neck with their winning responses. Simon's response is, *'Homelessness is a lifestyle choice'*. Judas thinks he has won with, *'Restore capital punishment'*, but is trumped by Jesus's response, *'Take away their televisions'*. Judas, already jealous of Jesus's popularity, is bitterly angry at losing.

The Resurrection of Jesus

Upon arrival to curry night, Jesus's friends bring him gifts. Matthew, a pharmacist, gives Jesus an elderberry potion. Peter, a chemical engineer, gives Jesus a synthetic resurrection stone called cubic boron nitride. Simon, a tech expert, gives Jesus an invisibility cloak made of lenticular sheets, which shines light at 10,000 angles to create hidden spots.

After the odious evening, Judas poisons Jesus's wine. Jesus' heart stops beating. His friends lay his dead body to rest in a cave along with their gifts.

The elderberry potion seeps into Jesus which causes retching and an adrenaline surge which causes his heart to beat. Jesus wakes suddenly.

He uses the cubic boron nitride to scratch the boulder blocking the cave, which causes it to roll slightly. He then uses the lenticular sheet fabric to escape without being seen. He leaves politics and goes quietly to live on a croft with lambs, chicks and bunnies.

Easter

Easter is celebrated in spring when lambs, chicks and bunnies are born. Not only are lambs, chicks and bunnies super cute but they also represent the animals that Jesus had on his croft.

At Easter time, Christians buy items that symbolise the resurrection of Jesus such as lambs, chicks, bunnies, boulders, paint for boulders, eggs, paint for eggs, chocolate, chocolate eggs, chocolate bunnies, invisibility cloaks, elderberries, greeting cards, baskets, chocolate baskets, cubic boron nitride and chocolate cubic boron nitride. Buying things makes Christians feel happy and chocolate is eaten because it is nice.

Biblical Aid

Old Testament

In the beginning, God makes the heavens and the Earth (day 1), day, night and sky (day 2), land (day 3), Sun, moon and stars (day 4), fish and birds (day 5), animals including humans (day 6), and chills (day 7).

Marriage is for companionship, procreation, and redemption. Spouses should love each other. Marriage should be between a man and woman.

Adam and Eve are the first humans and live in the Garden of Eden. God said not to eat apples. Eve eats an apple. God bans them from the garden.

Noah takes two of every animal on an ark to avoid floods and save each species.

A human race speak one language and almost build the Tower of Babel to the heavens. God thwarts their ambitions by destroying the tower, dispersing humans and enforcing a variety of languages upon them.

God promises Abraham and Sarah that they would have a son and when Sarah is 90, she does.

Abraham binds his son Isaac in preparation for child sacrifice upon God's orders. At the last minute, God withdraws his orders and reveals it was a test of loyalty. Isaac later marries his cousin Rebecca.

Jacob wants to marry Rachel. Her father tricks Jacob into marrying Leah first. He marries Rachel 7 years later. Jacob has two mistresses also.

Baby Moses is placed in a basket on the river Nile to save him from Egyptian persecution. Unknowingly, an Egyptian princess adopts him. She is referred to as Maris in some later Christian versions of the story.

The 10 plagues of Egypt for not freeing Israelites are: turning water to blood, frogs, lice, flies, cow disease, boils, hail, locusts, darkness and death of firstborn sons.

Samson's long hair gives him special strength, demonstrated by him killing a lion with his bare hands. Delilah seduces him, works this out, has a servant cut his hair and tells his enemies.

God talks through a burning bush to Moses about freeing Israelites.

The 10 commandments God gives Moses are: thou shalt only believe in me, not swear using my name, go to church on Sundays, honour parents, not kill, commit adultery, steal, lie, or covet thy neighbour's house or wife.

Moses leads the Israelites to freedom from Egypt. God helps by blowing wind that parts the Red Sea. The Egyptian army is drowned as they follow.

David, a shepherd boy, defeats the giant Goliath with only a slingshot and stone.

Praying to anyone but the king is forbidden. Daniel prays to God so is thrown in a Lion's Den. An angel is sent by God to hold the lions' mouths shut so Daniel is left unharmed.

Jonah does not fulfil God's ultimatum of preaching to the people of Nineveh within 40 days. A whale swallows Jonah for 3 days. Jonah then preaches to the people of Nineveh.

New Testament

The Virgin Mary is pregnant despite never having had sex. The Angel Gabriel tells her that it is God's baby.

The birth of Jesus takes place in a stable. Three wise men bring gifts of frankincense, gold and myrrh.

Christmas Day is Jesus's birthday. Starting around 800, Christmas becomes an increasingly popular celebration involving drinking, gambling, promiscuity, food and gifts. Christmas is banned for being immoral during the English republic 1647 – 1660.

John the Baptist preaches about God and baptises Jesus.

Jesus fasts in the desert for 40 days and 40 nights whilst the Devil tempts him to turn items into food. Jesus resists. Jesus is hungry afterwards.

Jesus turns 500 litres of water into wine at a wedding.

The Good Samaritan – A Jewish priest (high status) and Levite (high status) ignore a traveller who has been mugged, whilst a Samaritan (lower status) helps.

Jesus walks on water to a ship during a storm. Peter tries but fails due to a lack of faith. Jesus climbs aboard, the wind stops, and they sail to shore.

The Last Supper is when Judas betrays Jesus by disclosing his whereabouts to the Romans.

Good Friday is when Jesus is crucified. Good means holy in this instance.

Easter Sunday is when Jesus is reborn. He rises from the dead, escapes from a cave and then ascends to the sky. Easter is celebrated in spring because animals have lots of sex at this time, meaning many baby animals are born. This symbolises new life.

ABOUT THE AUTHOR

Rupert lives on planet Earth with his family and cats. He enjoys gardening, inexpensive red wine and putting the world to rights.

Have a delightfully interesting and biblical day!

Secret Version

The Resurrection of Jesus

Resurrection of Jesus

Judas has a tantrum after losing the card game and Jesus is fed of his constant complaining. Jesus is also fed up with the hypocrisy of politicians, whining constituents and being 'the people's' leader. He is fed up of dating and being rejected for lacking the nonchalant quality that is apparently so desirable.

So, Jesus goes on a massive bender. His beer goggles not only make everyone else more alluring but, make Jesus feel confident and empowered. He laughs, cries and dances. He shares secrets, intimacy and illicit substances with strangers.

A few days later, he agonisingly wakes up on a sofa with someone. Neither of them is as attractive as they were when they met.

Jesus's head is sore and his body is aching. He goes on a shaky walk and then crawls into a small cave to rest. His phone runs out of charge and his friends do not hear from him for days.

Jesus reassesses his life choices, leaves politics and goes to live on a croft with lambs, chicks and bunnies.

His followers concoct the earlier resurrection story because the truth is embarrassing and not ideal for founding a new religion.

Printed in Dunstable, United Kingdom

74502078R00049